ANDROCLES
AND
THE LION

ANDROCLES

an Aesop Fable

HOLIDAY HOUSE/NEW YORK

AND THE LION

adapted and illustrated by

JANET STEVENS

For LINDA

Library of Congress Cataloging-in-Publication Data

Stevens, Janet.
Androcles and the lion / adapted from Aesop and illustrated by
Janet Stevens. — 1st ed.
p.   cm.
Summary: A retelling of the Aesop fable describing the
consequences of the meeting between the slave Androcles and a
wounded lion.
ISBN 0-8234-0768-3
[1. Fables.]   I. Aesop.   II. Title.
PZ8.2.S835An   1989
398.2′452974428—dc19
[E]   89-1953   CIP   AC

ISBN 0-8234-0768-3
ISBN 0-8234-0906-6 (pbk.)

Once upon a time there was a slave called Androcles. He was owned by a master who was very cruel. He made Androcles work long hours in the hot sun. The master was also very fat. He made Androcles bring him heaping plates of food so he could stuff himself.

Androcles was gentle and kindhearted. After his hard work was done and his cruel master was fast asleep, the stray animals of the city came to visit.

Every night before falling to sleep, the cruel master remembered to shackle Androcles. But one night he forgot.

Androcles heard his master snoring. He hesitated
only a moment, then bolted out the door and ran
deep into the forest.

Androcles found a dry cave and made it his home.
Soon the animals of the forest became his friends.
His life was peaceful and happy.

One morning Androcles awoke to the sound of groaning and moaning near his cave. He tiptoed outside to see what was making the noise. He slowly approached the bushes.

R–R–R–R a fierce lion roared.

Androcles jumped straight up, then began scrambling for safety. As he turned to run, he noticed the lion's paw. It was swollen and bleeding. Androcles stopped. He thought, "Poor old fellow, no wonder he's roaring. That paw must hurt." He carefully walked closer to the lion and asked, "What happened to you, big guy?" The roar faded to a groan, and the lion held up his paw.

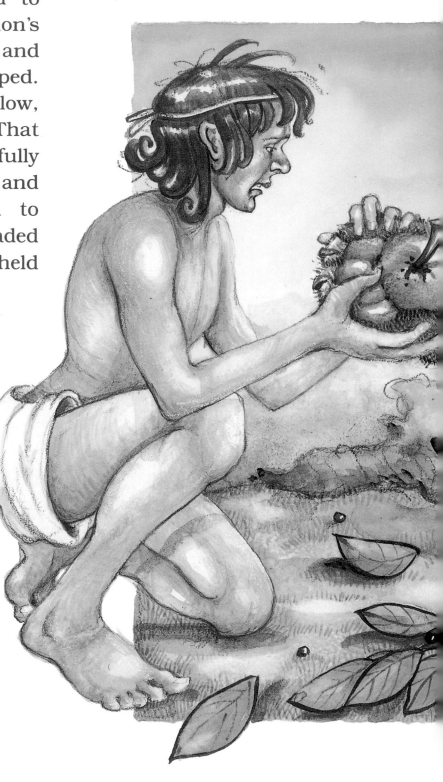

"Easy boy," said Androcles as he took a closer look. "Poor lion. There's a big nasty thorn stuck in your paw. Will you let me pull it out? Now be still and don't bite me." Androcles gently removed the thorn.

The lion felt much better. He licked Androcles'
hand to say thank you.

Then he rested awhile before limping away into the forest.

Meanwhile, the cruel master was very angry. He sent Roman soldiers to hunt for Androcles. They searched in the small villages, marched through the big cities, and finally rode into the forest. It was only a matter of time before the soldiers found Androcles. They dragged him from the cave and took him prisoner.

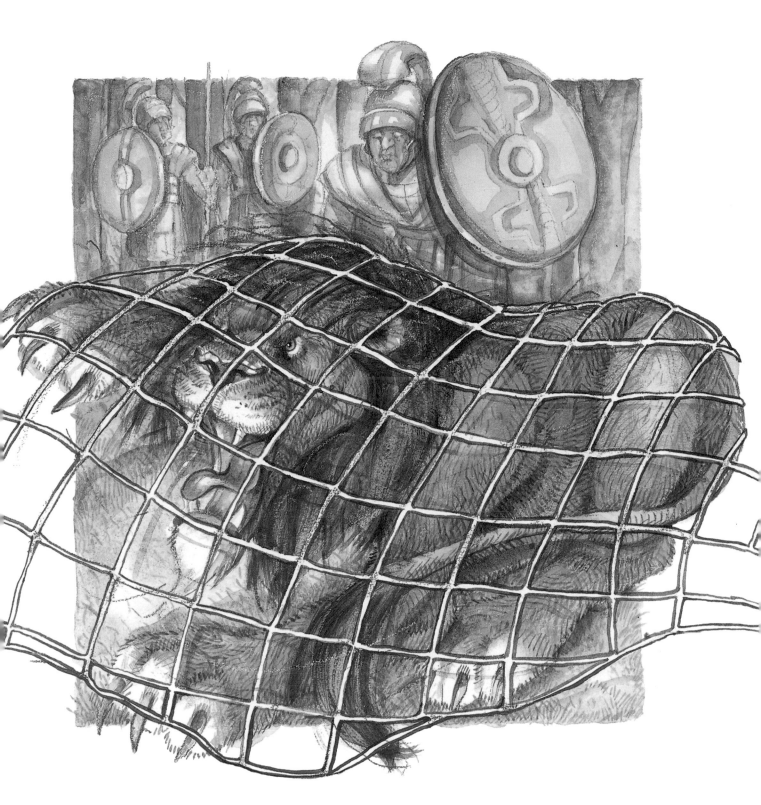

At the same time, another group of soldiers was hunting for animals in the forest. They came upon the lion. They dropped nets on him and carried him back to Rome.

The Roman judges gathered to decide what to do with the runaway slave, Androcles. A common punishment was to throw the prisoner to a hungry lion. If Androcles defeated the lion, he would be set free. If he didn't, he would be eaten. The judges decided Androcles should face the lion in the Colosseum.

They starved the lion for three days.

Then Androcles and the lion were brought to the arena. The crowd cheered, the lion roared, R–R–R–R, and Androcles shook with fear.

The Roman guard opened the lion's cage.

The lion raced out. He sprang high into the air. He showed his claws and roared. The crowd gasped. But ...just before pouncing on Androcles, the lion dropped to the ground.

He began purring and making happy noises. He started to lick Androcles' hand. Androcles smiled. He recognized the lion he had helped in the forest. Androcles reached out and took the lion's paw. The crowd cheered.

Androcles and the lion were set free. They lived happily ever after in the forest.

Androcles had learned an important lesson:

A noble soul never forgets a kindness.